MiPod XL

Welcome to the Forest, where
THE MINISTRY OF MONSTERS
helps humans and monsters live side
by side in peace and harmony...

CONNOR O'GOYLE
lives here too, with his gargoyle mum,
human dad and his dog, Trixie.
But Connor's no ordinary boy...

When monsters get out of control,
Connor's the one for the job.
He's half-monster, he's the Ministry's
NUMBER ONE AGENT,
and he's licensed to do things
no one else can do. He's...

MONSTER BOY!

For Nathaniel Bins

First published in 2009 by Orchard Books
First paperback publication in 2010

ORCHARD BOOKS
338 Euston Road, London NW1 3BH
Orchard Books Australia
Level 17/207 Kent St, Sydney, NSW 2000

ISBN 978 1 40830 242 2 (hardback)
ISBN 978 1 40830 250 7 (paperback)

Text and illustrations © Shoo Rayner 2009

The right of Shoo Rayner to be identified as the author and
illustrator of this work has been asserted by him in accordance with the
Copyright, Designs and Patents Act, 1988.

A CIP catalogue record for this book is available from the British Library.

1 3 5 7 9 10 8 6 4 2 (hardback)
1 3 5 7 9 10 8 6 4 2 (paperback)

Printed in Great Britain

Orchard Books is a division of Hachette Children's Books,
an Hachette UK company.

www.hachette.co.uk

MONSTER BOY

DRAGON DANGER

SHOO RAYNER

ORCHARD BOOKS

Showers of electric-blue sparks lit up the garage as Connor's mum worked on his latest and most exciting bike.

"There!" Mum switched off the welding torch and removed her mask. "Let's see if it works."

Connor wheeled the bike onto the grass in front of the Pedal-O bike shop where they lived. Except it wasn't an ordinary bike – it was a gyrocopter, an amazing flying bike that Mum had designed.

"The metal is really strong and very light," Mum explained. "But it needs an incredibly high temperature to weld the pieces together properly. I hope it holds firm."

Mum gave the rotor a spin. Trixie yapped in front of him as Connor pedalled down the runway.

"Take off!" Connor whooped as he lifted a few centimetres off the ground.

The gyrocopter creaked, groaned and split apart. Connor tumbled to the ground and landed heavily on his bottom.

"Ow!" he complained, rubbing his backside. "It's never going to work, Mum!"

"I need a much hotter welding torch," Mum sighed. "I don't know where I can get one."

Just then, Connor's MiPod beeped an emergency signal. He pulled the device out of his pocket and read the screen.

MISSION ALERT!

To:	Monster Boy, Number One Agent
From:	Mission Control, Ministry of Monsters
Subject:	Heat sensors near Murkwell Caves indicate fire hazard

Dragons are known to live in the area. Be careful – it's a favourite site for illegal rubbish dumping.

Please investigate immediately.

Good luck!

M.O.M.

THIS MESSAGE WILL SELF-ERASE IN FIFTEEN SECONDS

"I need MB4
right now,"
Connor ordered.

"I'll get it ready," said Mum. "You go
and put your fireproof clothes on."

MB4 FIREPROOF CLOTHING STORE

Minutes later, Connor was zooming off into the Forest. Trixie sat in the front basket, pointing out the way.

"Be careful!" Mum called after them.
"Yes, Mum!" Connor shouted.

Connor's mum was a Gargoyle, so Connor was half-monster. His code-name was Monster Boy. If anyone could look after himself, Connor could.

MONSTER BIKE INFO

MB4

MB4 is a firefighting bike.
Compressed CO_2 and bubble liquid create
huge amounts of foam. Foam starves fires
of oxygen, putting them out immediately.

MB4 has wide, high-traction tyres to
navigate the most inaccessible terrain.

MB4 carries breathing equipment,
rescue gear and a first-aid kit.

Murkwell Caves were an old and secret part of the Forest. The caves were ancient iron mines. Now they provided cool, safe retreats for many of the Forest's monsters.

Connor smelt the smoke before he saw it. MB4's power-assisted, wide-traction wheels allowed him to weave through the trees, crushing any obstacles in his way.

This *was* an emergency! A fire was burning fiercely. The lower branches of nearby trees were starting to smoke. If Connor couldn't put out the fire soon, the whole Forest might burn up!

Connor pulled
down his visor and
aimed the foam jets
at the fire. He turned
the safety-catch on
his handlebar to
"live" and pressed
the big red button.

With a deafening *whoosh*, clouds of white foam streamed out of MB4. The firefighting bubbles engulfed the flames and soon put an end to the danger.

Trixie barked a warning. Connor heard a loud, popping explosion. He snapped his head round in time to see a flash of blinding white light through the trees. Another fire had started.

Connor sprang into action and quickly had the new fire under control.

Trixie barked another warning. Connor followed her gaze...

"Oh! He's so cute!"
Connor grinned.

A baby Dragon, no more than a metre long, was curled up in the bracken. Its eyes scrunched up as an attack of hiccups sent ripples along its long, snaky body.

Without warning, the Dragon's stomach blew up like a balloon. There was a muffled *whump!* The little Dragon flicked its head and a blast of white-hot flame shot out of its flaring nostrils.

As the flame hit the ground, Connor was knocked clean off his feet and blown backwards into the bracken.

POP!

MiPOD MONSTER IDENTIFIER PROGRAM

Monster:	
Dragon	

Distinguishing Features:
Long scaly body and large nostrils.

Preferred Habitat:
Volcanoes.

Essential Information:
Dragons are not as dangerous as they once were. But they can still be a threat if they have swallowed toxic chemicals. Therefore do not mix Dragons and toxic chemicals.

It's always best to be polite to Dragons!

Danger Rating: 2

While he blinked his eyes back into focus, Connor's MiPod beeped again. It was a message from his dad, Gary O'Goyle, the world-famous Mountain Bike Champion.

"Oh, Dad!" Connor muttered. "You always send messages at the most unhelpful times!"

Hi son,

I won the Mount Fuji Mountain Bike Challenge!

Here's a picture. Phew! It sure is hot cycling up a volcano!

Lots of love,
Dad

"It's pretty hot here too, Dad," Connor muttered under his breath.

Trixie growled. Her eyes were wide with fear. Connor could see his own reflection in Trixie's visor. He could also see the reflection of something else...something very big!

Connor turned round
and found himself staring
into the cold, green eyes of
a fully grown and very
angry Dragon!

"What have you done to my little boy?" it growled. Connor felt the soft earth tremble beneath him and smelt the Dragon's awful breath.

"N-n-n-nothing, sir!" Connor replied, remembering that it's always best to be polite to Dragons. "I-I-I'm just here to put the fires out."

"Then you'd better get on with it before we all get cooked!" the Dragon roared.

"My Little Smokums says he ate something he found in a ditch," the big Dragon explained.

Little Smokums showed them where he had found some old barrels. On each barrel a skull and crossbones was printed in black on a bright-yellow sticker, along with the words "Toxic" and "Poison".

"How many times have I told you not to eat any old rubbish you find?" said the big Dragon.

Little Smokums hiccupped and hung his head.

Connor smiled. "It's not his fault. I blame the people who dumped the stuff. Anyway, I think Little Smokums might just be able to help me..."

"Here you are, Mum, try this!" Connor settled the little Dragon in front of the gyrocopter and showed him where the metal needed to be welded together.

Little Smokums scrunched up his eyes,
hiccupped and blasted a jet of white-hot
flame onto the metal.

"That's amazing!" gasped Mum. "It's a perfect join!"

PEDAL

"Let's test it out," Connor cheered, pulling off his firefighting kit.

Minutes later, Connor pedalled crazily down the grassy landing strip. He adjusted the rotor blades and the gyrocopter lifted up into the sky.

"Yahooo!" he yelled. "I'm flying, Mum!"

"Yap-hoo!"
Trixie barked.
She'd never been
flying with
Connor before.
It was fun!

"Yah-choo!"
exploded Little
Smokums, who
flew alongside,
flapping his tiny
wings like a
hummingbird.

As they raced across the sky, Little Smokums' explosions became quieter and quieter, until his fire was almost out.

Far below them, Connor watched the Ministry vans remove the barrels of waste that had been dumped at Murkwell Caves.

"What sort of stupid people dump dangerous stuff like that?" Connor wondered. "Anyone could get hurt."

Connor turned to the tiny dragon. "I think you can to go home now, Little Smokums. Remember to keep away from anything that looks like rubbish!"

Little Smokums
hiccupped one last time.
A wisp of smoke puffed
out of his nose as he
dived down to the
ground, where his father
was waiting for him.

SHOO RAYNER

MONSTER BOY

Dino Destroyer	978 1 40830 248 4
Mummy Menace	978 1 40830 249 1
Dragon Danger	978 1 40830 250 7
Werewolf Wail	978 1 40830 251 4
Gorgon Gaze	978 1 40830 252 1
Ogre Outrage	978 1 40830 253 8
Siren Spell	978 1 40830 254 5
Minotaur Maze	978 1 40830 255 2

All priced at £3.99

The Monster Boy stories are available from all good bookshops,
or can be ordered direct from the publisher:
Orchard Books, PO BOX 29, Douglas IM99 1BQ
Credit card orders please telephone 01624 836000
or fax 01624 837033 or visit our website: www.orchardbooks.co.uk
or e-mail: bookshop@enterprise.net for details.

To order please quote title, author and ISBN
and your full name and address.
Cheques and postal orders should be made payable to 'Bookpost plc.'
Postage and packing is FREE within the UK
(overseas customers should add £2.00 per book).

Prices and availability are subject to change.